WELCOME TO

Beast Quest

Collect the special coins in this book.
You will earn one gold coin for
every chapter you read.

Once you have finished all the chapters,
find out what to do with your gold coins at
the back of the book.

With special thanks to Allan Frewin Jones

For Rosie M, with gratitude

www.beastquest.co.uk

ORCHARD BOOKS
338 Euston Road, London NW1 3BH
Orchard Books Australia
Level 17/207 Kent St, Sydney, NSW 2000

A Paperback Original
First published in Great Britain in 2015

Beast Quest is a registered trademark of Beast Quest Limited
Series created by Beast Quest Limited, London

Text © Beast Quest Limited 2015
Cover and inside illustrations by Steve Sims
© Beast Quest Limited 2015

A CIP catalogue record for this book is available from
the British Library.

ISBN 978 1 40833 491 1

1 3 5 7 9 10 8 6 4 2

Printed and bound by CPI Group (UK) Ltd, Croydon, CR0 4YY

The paper and board used in this book are made from wood
from responsible sources.

Orchard Books is an imprint of Hachette Children's Group
and published by The Watts Publishing Group Limited,
an Hachette UK company.

www.hachette.co.uk

PLEXOR
THE RAGING REPTILE

BY ADAM BLADE

ORCHARD

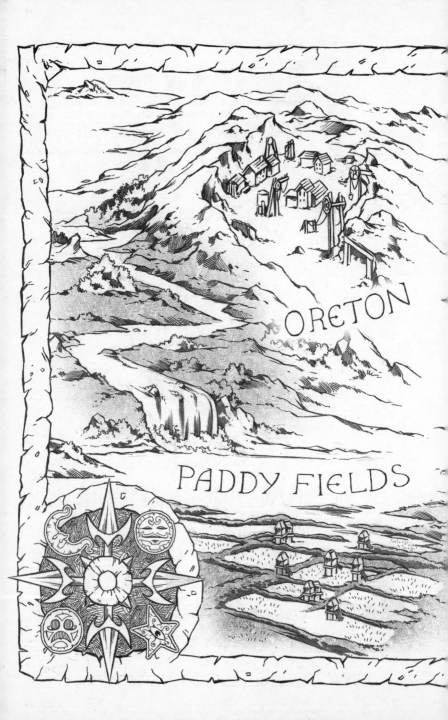

ORETON

PADDY FIELDS

CONTENTS

Dear Reader

You join us at a moment of great historical importance. King Hugo of Avantia is about to make an official visit to our neighbours in the south, the kingdom of Tangala. Tangala was once Avantia's staunchest ally, but the kingdoms have been at odds for decades. Now, the marriage of His Majesty to Tangala's Queen Aroha will unite our kingdoms once again.

Tangala is the only kingdom in which no Beasts lurk. Powerful ancient magic protects the kingdom's borders from Evil. It is our hope that this journey should be a simple one, untouched by danger...

But things are rarely so simple.

Aduro
Former Wizard to King Hugo

PROLOGUE

"I don't think we've been seen," Cory said, staring back to the harbour as he rowed their small boat into the middle of the lake. "Emiri, make sure the nets don't get tangled."

His sister gave him a nervous glance. "What if the Cursed Fish gets us?" she asked.

"There's no such thing!" Cory scoffed. "I'm more worried about getting caught fishing on the night before the Festival of the Rains – you know it's forbidden!"

All along the harbour that fronted their small village of mud huts, flags and bunting rippled in the wind. The fishing boats tied to the quays were also decorated, with bright banners on their masts. Cory had helped with the festival preparations. Like the rest of his village, he hoped the celebration would bring life-sustaining rain to the scorched desert that surrounded the oasis.

"But we must fish, or there'll be nothing to eat," said Emiri. She peered at her brother. "Why did the wells on our land go dry, Cory? I don't understand."

"No one knows why," he said.

Emiri stared up at the star-filled sky. "Father says that if the rains don't come soon, all our animals will die," she said softly.

"Check the nets," said Cory. "Let's see what we've caught."

Emiri leaned over the stern of the boat and dragged in the nets. "They're empty," she said, slumping onto the bench. "Not one fish!"

Then her eyes slid past Cory, widening in fear. She flung her hands up to her face and screamed.

Cory spun around. A great dark shape loomed towards them on the water, with a gaping, tooth-filled mouth and a great, staring eye. Cory caught his breath, his heart hammering against his ribs. But then he heard the clop of water against a wooden framework, and relief flooded his veins.

"It's only the model of the Cursed Fish!" he told his sister. "Look at it –

it's just timber and canvas. You saw the men making it two days ago."

Emiri pushed out her lower lip. "It took me by surprise, that's all," she muttered as Cory began to row away from the float. Each year, the villagers made a model for the celebrations. The following day, when the lake was full of boats, the villagers would throw their nets over the Cursed Fish and bring it ashore, just like the Great Hero did in the old legends. Then the feasting and dancing would start.

And hopefully the rains will come, thought Cory.

Emiri flung the net out once more and it sank quickly into the dark water. "Do you believe there really was a Cursed Fish once?" she asked.

"Of course not," said Cory, rolling his eyes. "It's just a silly old story."

The boat jerked suddenly and water splashed over the bows.

Cory leapt to the edge and stared into the water. "It must be a fish!" he cried, snatching at the net. "A really big fish! Help me haul it aboard!"

Emiri grabbed the net as well, grimacing as she pulled. But whatever was on the other end yanked so hard Cory lost his footing and was almost tipped out of the boat. As he braced his feet against the inside of the hull, something colossal moved just under the surface and Cory's blood turned to ice when he glimpsed a cruel eye staring up at him.

"Let go of the net!" he shouted to Emiri. "We have to get out of here."

They let the net slip away. Cory lunged for one oar, while the terrified-looking Emiri gripped hold of the other.

"What did you see?" she cried, as they struggled to turn the boat towards the shore. "Was it the real Cursed Fish?"

"I don't know!"

As they fought with the oars, a vast black shape reared up out of the lake, water cascading from its sides as it rose in front of them. Its monstrous head blotted out the stars.

An eye glared down at them, shining with greeny-gold light

that lit up a long scaly snout and a flickering red tongue, thin and deadly as a steel blade.

The monster wasn't a fish at all – it was a gigantic reptile!

The creature tossed its crested head, and the terrible eye stared at them. With a screech that seared itself into Cory's skull, the Beast lunged for them.

"Jump!" Cory shouted, catching hold of his sister as he flung himself headlong from the boat.

He heard the crunch of breaking timbers. Splintered wood was like a blizzard around them as the monster ripped the boat to fragments.

"Swim to the shore!" Cory yelled at his sister. But even as they struggled

in the churning water, a great
shadow fell over them.

Cory stared up in horror as a
gaping red mouth, filled with flesh-
shredding teeth, plunged down
towards them.

1

THE SEARING DESERT

"Keep going, Storm," said Tom, patting his horse's glistening neck. "We're almost at the oasis." He and Elenna trudged through the searing desert, Tom leading his black stallion by the reins. Even without Tom on his back, Storm was struggling in the heat.

We have to go on. The next Beast

must be vanquished.

Silver padded on ahead, his paws leaving deep marks in the fine sand, his tongue lolling from his mouth. Elenna wiped beads of sweat from her forehead as she examined the map of Tangala. Aroha, Queen of this southern land, had told them how the ancient map would lead them to the magical Treasures which protected the kingdom from Beasts. It was the only clue they had in their Quest to thwart the evil Wizard Velmal. When he had stolen the Treasures from the palace in the city of Pania, he had broken the spell which kept the Beasts away.

Tom glanced at the bag that hung from Storm's saddle. Already, he and his companions had managed to defeat two Beasts and take back the crown and the ring. But the orb and the sceptre were still missing.

It was bad enough that Velmal's actions had put the kingdom in peril, but Tom and Elenna were blamed for the theft, threatening to disrupt the planned marriage of King Hugo and Queen Aroha. Without the marriage, the longed-for treaty to restore the union between Avantia and Tangala would be doomed.

Tom knew that the only way he could prove he and Elenna were innocent, and prevent the two kingdoms coming into conflict, was to find the missing Treasures and take them back to the Palace.

Their Quests were made harder by the presence of Queen Aroha's nephew, Prince Rotu, who thought he was the right person to retrieve the lost Treasures. Tom thought the interfering prince was dangerously bigheaded – he'd do anything to claim glory for himself.

"The village of Aran isn't far away now," Elenna said, showing Tom the map. The village hugged the banks of a wide blue lake, looking very lonely in the vast wasteland of sand and scrub.

"That's good," said Tom. "We've almost run out of water now." He looked at Elenna. "Rotu is probably already in the village, stirring up trouble as usual."

"If he had any sense, he'd go back to Pania," said Elenna, kicking at the sand in frustration.

Tom understood her annoyance. Rotu had almost cost Silver his life on their last Quest. As they crossed Tangala's ferocious river, the prince

had cut the rope connecting their ferry to the shore, sending the boat tumbling over the waterfall – with Elenna's wolf still on board. Luckily Silver had survived the fall and returned to them.

They climbed the long, dusty ridge while the midday sun beat down, making the air shimmer.

Suddenly Tom stopped in his tracks, staring at a point in front of them where the haze gathered and became even more dense. "What is that?" he muttered.

He moved his hand to his sword hilt, preparing for danger.

A moment later, an image of

Daltec the good Wizard appeared in front of them, floating in the air.

The young Wizard's face was grey with worry. "I don't have much time," he gasped, his eyes flicking from left to right as though he was afraid of being overheard. "King Hugo and all the Avantians have been put under house arrest by Queen Aroha's special guard."

"Why would they do that?" demanded Tom.

"The High Council of Pania have accused us of helping you steal the kingdom's Treasures," Daltec said.

"Does the queen really believe that?" gasped Elenna.

Daltec's forehead wrinkled in anxiety. "Not completely, no – but she's beginning to have doubts." His voice lowered to a fierce whisper. "The councillors are even suggesting that the queen should declare war on Avantia."

"No!" cried Tom. "You have to find a way to get us more time to prove our innocence."

"I'll try." Daltec gave a shudder, his head turning and his eyes widening. "They're coming," he hissed. "I mustn't be caught using magic – they'll think I'm trying to weave a spell to help us escape." His image began to fade. "Only you can save us from war now, Tom – you must get the Treasures back!"

"I shall!" shouted Tom. "Tell the others not to worry – I won't let you down, I promise."

But the young Wizard had gone.

Elenna stared at Tom, her face pale with dread. "Do you think they'd attack Avantia?" she asked.

"Not if I can help it," Tom replied. "Come on, we need to get to the next Beast as quickly as possible."

Tom led the others in the direction of Aran, ignoring his aching legs. But the endless desert seemed to go on forever. They had been trekking for what seemed like an age when Tom heard a noise that made him suddenly halt. He raised his hand to the others. Then he heard it again – a desperate cry ringing out again from

just beyond the crest of the ridge.

"What's that?" said Elenna.

"Someone is in trouble," replied
Tom, drawing his sword and running
on ahead. He crested the hill and
saw a well among the rocks.

A figure lay beside the well, face

down, half buried in the sand.

Tom leaped wildly down the hillside, determined to get to the collapsed figure. He dropped to his knees, reaching out quickly to turn the person onto his back.

His heart lurched as he realised who it was.

Rotu!

31

SUNSTROKE!

"Water!" rasped the prince as Tom helped him to sit up.

Tom saw Elenna coming over the hill. "Fetch water," he called.

Elenna strode forward with their water skin. "What happened?" she asked bluntly, as the prince snatched the skin out of her hands.

"Drink sparingly," Tom told him. "It's all we have till we reach Aran."

The prince gulped the water
greedily. Tom felt prickles of
annoyance, as most of their precious
water vanished down Rotu's throat.
He needs it more than we do...
The prince wiped his mouth and

handed the skin back to Elenna. He got shakily to his feet. "Thank you," he said. "I thought this well would be full, but it's run dry." He gave them a shamefaced look. "I should have stayed with you instead of racing on ahead. I've been an arrogant fool."

Tom might not have trusted Rotu, but he was glad they had found him before he'd died of thirst. At least now they could keep an eye on him.

"We should get moving," said Rotu. "I've lost track of how far it is."

"According to the map, there's an oasis not too far away," said Elenna, staring south where the land was creased into a series of ridges. "Just beyond those hills, I would think."

"Could I have a drop more water,

please?" asked Rotu. "I'm feeling a little faint in this heat."

Elenna gave him the water skin again and he drank while she and Tom examined the map.

"I think this is where we are," Elenna said, pointing to a small mark on the map. "We ought to be able to see the village soon."

"A girl reading a map," said Rotu, looking over Tom's shoulder. "Do you really trust her to guide you?"

"Please do pick a route if you don't think I can do it," Elenna said.

"I'm sure you know what you're doing," said the prince, handing Tom the water skin. "Take a drink before we get going."

"Thanks," said Tom, lifting the skin

and allowing himself a small sip of water before passing it to Elenna.

They made their way down the hillside and up the next ridge, Silver padding along ahead, panting.

A sudden wave of nausea made Tom feel dizzy. "Is the heat getting worse?" he asked, wiping his forehead. His head spun and the landscape shifted in front of his eyes.

"Would you like some more water?" Tom spun at the sound of the voice. An impossible figure was standing there behind him, holding out the water skin. It was a powerfully built man with a heavy moustache and thick brown hair. He was wearing a stained leather apron, and holding a blacksmith's hammer in one hand.

"Uncle Henry?" Tom gasped. "How did you get here?"

"The same way that I did," said a thin voice, and Tom turned again to see his own shadow turning cartwheels through the sand.

"No!" Tom gasped, stumbling

forwards. "This isn't right!"

"It's as right as rain!" said a
sneering voice and Tom saw the
witch Kensa standing in front of him
with her arms folded and a crooked
grin on her face. She pointed to
something behind Tom. "Take a look

over there, little hero," she taunted.

"Tom! Help me!"

Gasping, Tom turned to see his mother, Freya, standing on a rocky outcrop, her arms held out towards him, her face pleading.

"Mother?" he cried, staggering forwards. *What is she doing here? She should be in Gwildor!*

"Velmal has captured me again," cried his mother. "Only you can set me free." But as Tom stumbled towards her, her shape drifted through the rocks.

"I'm coming!" he gasped, gathering all the power that remained in his limbs to lunge after her floating image. Just as he snatched at his mother's hands, he felt something crash into him and knock him to the ground. He lay there panting and disorientated, but the shock had restored his vision. Storm's head pushed against his shoulder.

"What are you doing, Storm?" Tom said, trying to focus. The horse was nudging him and whinnying. He caught the reins and Storm lifted his head to help Tom to his feet.

"Mother?" He stared around, but the image of Freya was gone.

Then he saw the peril that Storm had saved him from. Only a couple of paces away, the rocky outcrop ended in a sheer fall into a deep ravine. What had happened to him?

I've got sunstroke! It's making me see things that aren't real. If Storm hadn't stopped me, I'd be lying down there! A sudden fear filled Tom. *What if Elenna and Rotu have the same problem? They could be in trouble.*

He ran back the way he had come, the loose sand making every step an ordeal. Sweat poured into his eyes.

I have to get to them!

Elenna was standing on a large rock, firing arrow after arrow off into the empty desert while Silver ran around the rock, howling in panic.

"Elenna!" Tom called, scrambling up onto the rock, ducking to avoid the flying arrows.

"They're coming from all sides!" Elenna shouted, her eyes wild as she shot arrows at nothing.

Tom picked up the water skin from

where Elenna had thrown it down. He uncorked it and flung the last of the water into her face. She let out a cry and collapsed into his arms.

A few moments later, she opened her eyes. "What happened?" she asked. "Where are Sanpao's pirates?"

"You were hallucinating," said Tom. "It must have been the lack of water and the heat." He stared at the empty water skin. "And now we have nothing left to drink." He frowned.

Where's Rotu?

Elenna ran her hands over her tunic, her eyes suddenly widening. "The map is missing," she gasped. "I must have dropped it. What will we do, Tom? Without the map, we're completely lost out here!"

3

ALL WHO ENTER MY WATERS WILL DIE!

"We have to find Rotu," Tom said. "If he's seeing things that aren't there, he could be in danger too."

They scoured the ground for any sign of tracks, but there were none.

"Silver will be able to follow his scent," said Elenna, her voice quavering slightly. She still seemed upset from losing the map, but beckoned the wolf over. "Silver – find the prince," she said.

The wolf ran backwards and forwards across the ridge, his muzzle close to the ground. But after a while, the animal came back to Elenna, looking up at her with apologetic eyes.

"Silver is always able to pick up a trail," Elenna said to Tom. "I don't understand it."

It doesn't make any sense, thought Tom. He cast frantic glances about the desert. The prince could be anywhere. "We can't just chase about, hoping to find him," he said. "But we can't abandon him either."

"We have no water," Elenna reminded him. "And without the

map, we'll be lucky even to find the oasis at Aran."

A thought struck Tom. "The red jewel!" he said, touching the gem set into his belt. "If the Beast we're searching for is near Aran, I might be able to hear its thoughts."

"Good plan," said Elenna. "The Beast will lead us to the village. We can get food and water there and lead a search party out into the desert to find Rotu."

Tom ran to the highest point on the ridge, closing his eyes, his hand on the jewel. He tried to clear his mind of all thoughts.

He still felt a little dizzy as he tried

to focus on any faint sounds that reached him.

At last, he heard a faint murmuring in his mind.

All who enter my waters will die!

He felt a shudder run down his spine, but opened his eyes, pointing to where he thought the voice was coming from.

"Are you sure?" asked Elenna.

"Not completely," Tom admitted. "And if I'm wrong, we could die of thirst out here."

"I trust you," said Elenna.

As they plodded on, they saw bleached bones lying in the sand. Many of them were scattered beside dried-up wells, as though the poor animals had gathered there as a last hope before dying.

"If all these wells are dry, perhaps the oasis is gone too," said Elenna.

They crested another barren ridge, and at last Tom saw the land fall away towards a great lake. His spirits rose. Lush grasses and tall

trees surrounded the clear blue
water. Even the air smelled sweeter.

We came the right way!

He gazed down at a village of
baked mud houses huddling close to
the lake. Fishing vessels floated in
the harbour, their masts bright with
colourful pennants and flags.

"Aran, at last!" cried Elenna.

"And it looks as though the people
are celebrating something," said
Tom. The power of his golden helmet
allowed him to see that the streets
were festooned with garlands, and
full of men, women and children in
strange costumes.

They made their way down the
hillside and into the village, the
desert giving way to palm trees

and the scent of the greenery. Up close, the costumes and masks worn by the people seemed much more outlandish and grotesque.

"They look like horribly deformed fish," Elenna murmured.

Tom came to a sudden halt, staring through the chanting crowds at a familiar figure. "It's Rotu!"

The prince was wandering among the people, smiling and nodding. His hair had been brushed and his clothes were pristine.

"Rotu!" Tom called.

The prince spun around, staring at them with a startled expression. For a moment, Tom thought that the young man was about to dart off. But then a relieved smile broke across his face as he came towards them.

"I'm so glad to see you," he said. "I had the most terrible hallucinations. I was in a daze for a long time. Then I passed out." He gave them an urgent look. "I looked everywhere for you when I woke up, but you were nowhere to be found, so I carried on walking and ended up here."

"We think it was the heat," said Elenna. "But at least we're safe now."

Not that safe, thought Tom, remembering the threat made by the Beast. He was about to say as much when a boy ran up to them, closely followed by a younger girl.

"You have to get out of here!" the

boy cried as he reached them. He and the girl were the only locals not wearing masks, and their faces were full of fear. He gestured at the people. "We tried to warn them, but nobody will listen to us."

"And who exactly are you, little fellow?" asked the prince in his most haughty voice.

"I'm Cory," said the boy. "And this is my sister, Emiri."

"We saw you before," said the girl, peering up at Rotu. "Where has your father gone?"

"What are you talking about?" snapped Rotu. But Tom noted a glint of panic in his eyes. "Don't you peasants know who I am?" Rotu went on. He smacked his hand to his chest.

"I am Prince Rotu, great-nephew to King Hura, praise his beloved memory!" He glared at the two children. "I arrived here alone."

Tom saw that the two children looked puzzled at this.

"Could you tell us what you're celebrating?" Rotu asked them.

"It's the annual Festival of the Rains," Cory said. "The wells around the lake have been dry for so many months now, that we're more desperate than ever for the rains to come. But if the boats go out on the lake, they'll all be destroyed."

"They're supposed to catch a model of the Cursed Fish," Emiri added eagerly.

"That's what brings the rains. But

there's a real monster out there," said Cory. "A huge reptile!"

"We tried to tell the grown-ups," said Emiri, her eyes filling with terror. "But they think we're imagining things."

A tall man in an especially fearsome fish mask approached them. "What's this, Cory and Emiri telling their silly tales again?" He wagged a finger at them. "You should know better than to frighten strangers with your tall stories." He turned to Tom and the others. "I am Hamran, Chief Elder of Aran," he said. "Welcome to our festival."

"You should listen to them," Tom said urgently. "Your village is in terrible danger."

"Nonsense," said Hamran. "The festival will continue." He laughed. "There are no monsters in the lake! Besides, it's too late." He pointed to the harbour, where the flotilla of boats was already starting to cast off.

Tom watched the boats with alarm.

"You have to stop them," he cried.
"If your people go out into the lake,
they'll all die!"

4

THE POWER OF THE BEAST

The village chief stared at Tom for a moment, then burst out laughing. "I see you're as gullible as these two children," he said. "They saw shadows and thought they were monsters – and you believe their stories! Well, have it your own way." He turned and marched into the crowds. "Come, good folk of Aran, gather at the harbour! The boats are setting off for the catching of the Cursed Fish!"

"Now what?" asked Elenna.

"We have to get to the harbour and do our best to stop them!" said Tom.

Tom and Elenna ran down to the lake, Rotu on their heels, along with Storm and Silver. Some of the fishermen were carrying painted harpoons, and others were stretching a huge net between several vessels.

In the middle of the lake, Tom could see something bobbing on the water. It seemed to be a large wooden frame covered in canvas, painted to resemble a fearsome fish.

"That's the model of the Cursed Fish," Cory said, pointing. "The old stories say that a real cursed fish lived out there, long ago."

"A mighty hero caught it and brought it ashore," said Emiri. "And that was when the rains came."

Tom ran to the end of one of the jetties. He cupped his hands around his mouth. "Turn back," he called to the fishermen. "You're in terrible danger, all of you!"

A few heard him, but they laughed. Before he could call again, the masked villagers along the harbour began to sing loudly, as they watched the boats glide towards the model of the Cursed Fish.

The Beast's cruel voice echoed

around Tom's head.

I shall drown every one of them!

"I need to get out there," Tom cried. "If I can't stop them, at least I can defend them against the Beast!"

"There's a boat over there," Cory said, gesturing to a small vessel by the jetty.

Tom ran to the boat, but the singing villagers barred his way.

"I need to get aboard," Tom said, trying to push past them.

"No stranger may take part in the ritual," said one man, his face hidden behind an ugly fish mask.

Silver padded up behind Tom, his teeth bared as he growled. The villagers retreated, stumbling back from the wolf. Storm too, came

pushing through the villagers,
stamping his hooves and jostling
them out of the way.

Tom and Elenna jumped into the
boat. Tom noticed a harpoon lying in
the bottom. "Rotu – you stay ashore,"
Tom called as he cast off. "Look after

Storm and Silver. We'll try to get to the Beast before it attacks!"

"Good luck," called Rotu as Tom grabbed the oars and began to row.

Elenna grasped the rudder and steered as Tom plied the oars. The strength from his golden breastplate allowed him to drive the blades into the water and sent the boat flying across the surface of the lake. Within moments they were halfway to the fleet of fishing boats.

Ahead, the water roiled and churned. With terrifying speed, a great, dark reptilian head burst out of the water among the boats, rocking them wildly. Some vessels turned over, and Tom could see their helpless crews in the water.

Tom heard the singing of the villagers on the shoreline turn to shouts and wails of terror as the Beast's long, sinuous neck bent, long jaws snapping at the boat closest to it. Fishermen leaped for safety as the creature's knife-sharp teeth clashed together, crunching their boats into splinters...

Tom stared up at the rearing Beast, its sleek flank and vast flippers lined with shining scales, its great mouth gaping to bite down on another helpless boat. Its right eye shone with a strange, greeny-gold light. Under the Beast's jaws, Tom saw feathery gills opening and closing.

"It can breathe in water and air!"
he called. "And do you see its eye?"

"It's the orb of Pania!" cried
Elenna. "The third of the lost
Treasures of Tangala!"

Tom redoubled his efforts on the

oars, and the boat skimmed over the water, heading straight for the roaring Beast.

He heard screams and shouts from the fishermen. "The Cursed Fish has come! We're all going to die!"

But a louder and more deadly voice reverberated deep inside Tom's head.

I am no fish, you fools! I am Plexor!

The Beast loomed higher out of the lake, ready to strike down on the stranded fisherman swimming frantically for the shore. Those still in their boats were rowing wildly to get away, but they wouldn't stand a chance if the Beast gave chase.

Tom heaved on the oars again, but their small boat was still too far away for him to strike Plexor.

Elenna stood up and loosed an arrow. The shaft cut through the air, striking the Beast's long neck, but glancing off its scales.

Plexor turned to them, his mouth gaping as he let out a scream of pure rage. Tom released the oars and stood at the prow of the boat, pressing his hand to the red jewel.

Leave those people alone!

Voices cried out from the water. "Help us! Please!"

"I have to go to them," exclaimed Elenna, snatching at the oars and rowing the boat towards a group of helpless people.

Who are you to make demands of me? Plexor's voice echoed around Tom's head, making him reel. *This lake is my domain!*

You can live in peace with the fishermen, Tom replied, staring up at the Beast.

No! came the reply. *Never! I have blocked the channels that feed water to the people's wells. Even if they remain on land, not one human will survive my wrath!*

Tom drew his sword and brandished it at the Beast.

"Hear me, Plexor!" he shouted aloud. "I am Avantia's Master of the Beasts. While there is blood in my veins, I will protect these people from you!"

5

ROTU THE HERO

"Tom – use the harpoon!" shouted Elenna, pointing to the deck.

Tom grabbed the weapon then jumped back onto the prow, reeling out the rope that attached the harpoon to the bows of the boat. He balanced himself as he brought his arm back, then carefully took aim at Plexor's head.

He flung the harpoon with all the

strength given to him by the golden breastplate. He watched as the rope snaked out through the air.

Plexor was huge, but he could move with the speed of a striking serpent. His neck coiled as he twisted and caught the harpoon in his teeth, his eyes burning. Plexor pulled back sharply on the rope, making the boat jerk through the water. Tom toppled backwards, crashing into Elenna as the Beast dragged the small boat through the water towards him.

Tom scrambled to his feet, spreading his arms for balance. He bent his knees and used the power of the golden boots to leap high into the air. At the highest point of the

jump, he drew his shield off his back
and angled his body so that he came
plummeting down towards the Beast.

He slammed the shield into the
side of Plexor's head, his own
shoulders jarring from the impact.

With a screech of anger and pain, Plexor let the harpoon fall from between his fangs and the little boat glided free with Elenna already plying the oars.

Tom wrapped his arms around the Beast's thick neck and slid downwards. Plexor shook himself, his rippling muscles breaking Tom's grip and sending him tumbling helplessly through the air.

Tom hit the surface of the lake and was swallowed by the seething water. Dizzy from his fall, he sank deeper and deeper. He stared up in alarm as the massive Beast churned through the water above him.

The sudden surge of the Beast's wake tossed him over and over. Tom fought against the turmoil, kicking hard to get upright again. Eventually he stabilised, pushing himself up to the surface. He took a gulp of air and looked around at the carnage, hoping to see some sign of the Beast.

A few people were still left swimming through the destruction, heading desperately for dry land.

Plexor was gone.

I have to find the Beast before...

Tom felt a great surge of water from beneath him.

He stared down into the water, startled to see Plexor powering up straight towards him. The Beast's wide jaws were gaping, his fangs like knives, his one real eye filled with hatred and vengeance.

Tom had only an instant to act. He threw himself towards a floating piece of timber, a moment before the jaws snapped shut right where he had been swimming. Tom scrambled up onto the plank. Floating pieces of debris stretched all the way back to the shore.

Already the Beast was searing through the water towards him once again. Tom jumped forwards onto another piece of timber, just as the Beast's teeth crunched the plank behind him into splinters.

Using his momentum, Tom leapt again, landing on another piece of floating debris, before springing for the next, like stepping stones. Plexor's screeches filled his ears, and the water was churning as the furious Beast pursued him, snapping his footholds to matchwood.

At every step, Plexor's jaws came closer, but with one final great leap, Tom sailed forwards and came crashing down in the soft mud at the lake's shore.

He sprang up, drew his sword and turned to face the Beast. Plexor rose up, his eyes blazing, and Tom prepared himself for a fight to the death.

Whooosshh!

Something long and slender cut through the air towards the Beast.

Clang!

As Tom watched, it struck off the back of Plexor's neck.

A harpoon!

The Beast twisted around, screeching.

Tom stared in alarm – the harpoon had come from a small boat in the middle of the lake. Rotu was standing at the prow.

"Foul Beast!" Rotu shouted. "Come – attack me if you dare!"

Tom saw a small flotilla of fishing boats backing Rotu up. The big net was stretched between them, and they were rowing towards the Beast.

That net won't be strong enough to hold a Beast as powerful as Plexor.

"No!" Tom shouted wildly. "Leave it to me! You'll all be killed."

Tom waded into the shallows.
"Plexor! Leave those men alone – I
am your enemy!" he shouted.

But the terrible Beast turned and
swam ferociously towards the small
group of doomed vessels. Tom hardly
dared to watch. Any moment now,
those great jaws would begin to
champ and men would die.

But as Plexor drew closer to the
boats, he slowed down, his long neck
sinking under the waves so that his
head was no higher than the masts of
the fishing boats.

As he closed in on Rotu's boat,
the Beast almost came to a halt, his
terrible teeth gnashing and his limbs
churning the water.

Why is Plexor hesitating? Tom

wondered. *Perhaps my blow to the side of his head did more damage than I thought.*

"Get away while you still can!" he shouted to Rotu.

"I defy you, Beast!" yelled the

prince, standing proudly in his boat as Plexor slowly approached him.

Plexor's head lifted, water splashing down over Rotu as the jaws gaped.

"Now, good people!" Rotu shouted.

The other boats closed in and the men flung the net over Plexor's head. Rotu grabbed at the trailing end of the net and yanked it hard, rocking back on his heels as the net tightened over the huge Beast.

Impossible! Tom stared in astonishment as Plexor struggled to get free. *The Beast must be exhausted or wounded.*

"Hold the Beast fast!" shouted Rotu. "Bring him to the shore!"

Tom could hardly believe his eyes

as the boats began to move gradually towards him, dragging the Beast along with them.

Rotu had saved the day.

"Well done!" cried Tom as the boats hit the shore. Plexor looked dull-eyed and defeated in the tangles of the net.

Rotu jumped ashore, dragging the strings of the net behind him and tying them firmly around the stump of a tree.

He turned to Tom, a triumphant grin on his face.

"I have served the Beast up to you like a festival roast!" he crowed. "But I cannot inflict its final defeat alone." His eyes gleamed. "Come, Avantian – let us finish this Quest together!"

Tom turned to Plexor and saw that the Beast was wallowing helplessly in the shallows.

All he had to do now was force the Beast to give up the orb and this part of his Quest would be done.

Could it really be so easy?

DEADLY DECEIT

Tom gripped his sword as he waded into the lake. Plexor eyed him with hatred through the net, but the Beast's long tail whipped only feebly in the water. Tom caught a movement in the corner of his eye. He thought for a moment that he saw a hooded and cloaked figure in a clump of palm trees at the lake's edge.

One of the villagers? But why would

a villager be hiding? And why did Tom think he seemed…familiar?

A loud splash brought Tom's attention back to the Beast. Plexor was lashing his tail more violently in the water now. As Tom waded waist-deep into the lake, Plexor's one real eye continued to watch him with cruel loathing.

"Be careful," cried Elenna.

Tom glanced back, seeing her on the shore a little way off, surrounded by grateful fishermen. She had her bow ready, an arrow trained on Plexor.

Tom faced the subdued Beast. Plexor still gnashed his vicious teeth together, as though wishing he could bite into Tom's flesh.

Using the feathery gills as

handholds, Tom clambered up onto the Beast's head. He stood sure-footed on the huge skull, drawing his sword with one hand, touching the red jewel with the other. Just below his right foot, the orb of Pania glowed eerily in the Beast's eye socket.

Do you submit, Plexor? he asked.

The Raging Reptile's voice rang in his head. *I submit...*

Tom lowered his sword, relieved that the fight was over almost before it had begun.

The voice in his head rose to a shrill roar: *...to no one!*

With a sudden surge and a deafening screech of triumph, Plexor lifted his head, bursting out of the net and rising high above the lake while

Tom struggled to keep to his feet.

Plexor's been faking weakness! The Beast's submission had just been a ruse to throw Tom off his guard. And it had worked!

Plexor snapped his head around. Tom's feet slid on the smooth scales

and he found himself tumbling through the air.

As he fell, the Beast's jaws opened, the dreadful stench of his foul breath filling Tom's nostrils as he fell right into the reptile's gaping mouth. Then the long fangs snapped shut behind

him like prison bars.

Immediately, Plexor's whipping tongue smashed Tom from side to side inside the cavernous mouth as the jaws opened and closed. Tom thrust his shield against the teeth, fear racing through him at the thought of those razor-sharp fangs cutting him in two.

I have to get out of here!

Desperately, Tom clawed his way to the front of the Beast's mouth, stamping down on the writhing tongue. He dropped onto his back, raising his legs and harnessing the power of the Golden Armour to help himself brace his feet against the roof of Plexor's mouth.

His legs shook, the muscles screaming from the effort as he gradually forced Plexor's jaws apart. Mucus sprayed over him from the Beast's yawning throat, and he could barely breathe for the stench of Plexor's breath.

But Tom held firm, prising the Beast's mouth open even wider, readying himself for the moment when he could fling himself clear.

He felt a rush of wind as Plexor's head plunged down towards the lake. Tom took a deep breath as the water rose to engulf him. Plexor dived and twisted, trying to dislodge Tom.

Disorientated, Tom slid from

the Beast's tongue. He felt the fangs graze his flesh, tearing at his clothes as he was thrown out of the mouth. Before Tom knew what was happening, the thick tail swung round, striking him with vicious force. Dizzy with pain, he spun downwards towards the depths, hardly able to keep a grip on his sword and shield.

He heard Plexor's voice in his head. *You will never defeat me!*

Tom hit the bottom of the lake, bubbles bursting from his mouth. He twisted around, then he kicked off from the lakebed and rose up through the seething water.

Tom stared around, the power of the golden helmet allowing his eyes to pierce the gloom of the deep water. The Beast was gone!

Tom came to the surface, gulping in air. There was no sign of Plexor.

How could I have fallen for such an obvious trick?

He had survived the fight, but he was still no closer to retrieving the Orb of Tangala.

Tom struck for the shore. More villagers were gathered at the shoreline as he waded out onto dry land. Hamran, the village chief, was there, with his mask clutched under his arm. His wrinkled face was grim.

"I thought you were a true hero," Hamran said, amid the murmurs of the disappointed-looking fishermen. "You let Prince Rotu down! He caught the Cursed Fish for you and put it at your mercy – and then you let it escape!"

"Now the rains will never come!" cried another man. "You have doomed us all!"

"Tom was braver than any of you!" piped a boy's voice, as Cory pushed his way through the crowd. "The monster played a sly trick that would have fooled anyone!"

Tom smiled gratefully at the boy, but he knew he should not have been caught out so easily.

"We will have to leave the village," said another man. "The wells will never run again – and we are

doomed if we stay here."

"Do not leave," cried Tom,
squaring his shoulders. "The Beast
is trying to drive you away. It's

Plexor that has blocked your wells and caused the drought."

The villagers looked at him, their faces doubtful.

A distant screeching cut across the lake. Plexor was gliding among the broken boats, his head raised as he let out his fearsome cries.

"The Beast is returning!" screamed one of the frightened villagers. "We must flee!"

"Stay!" shouted Tom. "Trust in me! I will go down into one of your wells, and I will follow the underground channel to the Beast's lair. I swear to you, I will defeat it!"

The villagers huddled together as Tom held his sword high.

"Give me this one last chance," he

cried. "You have my word of honour, your wells will run free again! I will not fail you!"

FLOODWATERS

Elenna and Rotu were at Tom's side as he strode out of the village and up the long hill to the nearest of the dry wells. Tom had left Storm and Silver in the safekeeping of Cory and his sister. His plan was to enter the well – neither horse nor wolf would be able to accompany him there.

"It's such a shame the Beast managed to trick you like that," said

Rotu in a smug voice. "After all the trouble I took to catch him. Who knew Beasts could be so cunning?"

"You didn't catch him," snapped Elenna. "Plexor let himself be caught so he could lure Tom close enough to be killed."

"If you say so," said Rotu with a dismissive wave of his arm. "If you want my opinion, Tom gave the Beast too much time to recover."

"Here's the well," Tom said grimly, trying not to let Rotu's barbs get to him. "Let the rope down, Rotu."

Rotu uncoiled the length of rope they had brought with them and dangled the end into the mouth of the dry well. The top end of the rope was secured around a large boulder.

"Keep your wits about you down there," said Elenna. "Plexor is crafty."

"Don't worry," said Tom, climbing onto the stone lip of the well. "I won't be fooled again."

He used the rope to let himself down into the well, the heat of the

day gradually making way for a
musty coolness as he descended.
His feet hit the well's dry bottom
and he stepped cautiously into the
great shaft that jutted away towards
the lake. Strands of dried weed
hung from the curved roof and the
shells of small molluscs crunched
underfoot as Tom made his way
along the shaft.

The grey rock was streaked with
crystal that shone with an eerie
blue-white light. With the powerful
vision gifted by the golden helmet,
Tom found he was able to see enough
to follow the dipping tunnel.

After a while, the occasional drip

oozed from the roof and formed small wet patches on the parched floor. It was hard to imagine that this dry hole had once been full of rushing water.

Tom slowed, listening intently, in the darkness, his every sense on highest alert. A curious sound drifted along the passageway. If he had been above ground, Tom would have imagined it to be distant thunder.

What is that?

He paused, tilting his head, trying to make sense of the faint sound as it grew gradually louder. The ground trembled under his feet as the noise increased. The tunnel took a bend just ahead of him, and now he finally knew what he was hearing!

Water! A lot of water!

The Beast roared in Tom's mind. *You cannot defeat me, so-called Master of the Beasts. You will drown!*

A moment later a huge torrent of lake water surged around the bend, foaming and boiling with the force of a tsunami. Tom braced himself for the impact, holding his shield up. Would the power of Sepron's tooth help him to survive the explosion of released water?

Slam! The jet of water hit him like a battering ram. Tom forced his shoulder into the shield, his head down, his feet planted firmly as the water surged around him. It nearly took him off his feet as it roared and howled and hissed and spat.

But his shield held firm. With a
pounding heart he began to forge
forwards against the weight of water.
His legs shook with the effort as,
step by step, he pushed towards the
opening to the oasis. Soon he could
barely breathe, and his strength was

ebbing – a few more moments of this and he would be swept off his feet.

No! Plexor will not defeat me!

But as the tunnel filled, the water level almost up to his head, the torrent slowed. Through the flowing water, Tom could just make out the entrance to the lake. New hope filled him and he waded on. He stretched up with his mouth to the sliver of air left at the top of the tunnel.

Taking a huge breath, Tom flexed his knees and kicked off, gliding upwards into the dark hole at the tunnel's end. He came out into the depths of the lake. Boulders scattered the oasis floor.

Those rocks must have been blocking the tunnel!

Looking up, Tom saw that the surface was far above him. He swam along the lake's bottom, saving his strength, calming himself so that his hammering heart slowed.

He used his enhanced eyesight to search the murky waters for any sign of the Beast.

His gaze snapped upwards. Plexor's long, lithe shape moved slowly among the drifting shards of the smashed boats on the surface.

He thinks I'm dead, Tom thought with grim satisfaction.

His eyes narrowed, his mind focused on the coming conflict.

Beware, Plexor! Now I have you just where I want!

RIDING THE BEAST

Tom was about to head for the surface when he spotted an anchor jutting up from the lakebed, trailing a rusty chain.

If I can get it loose, that chain may help me to bind Plexor.

Tom swam quickly downwards and, bracing his feet against the anchor, he gripped the chain and ripped it free.

His lungs were burning now from the effort of holding his breath. He needed air! He kicked upwards. The weight of the chain dragged on his arms, but the golden breastplate gave him the strength he needed to swim for the surface.

The lack of air was like an iron band tightening around his chest, but he kept below the surface, treading water. His head was spinning as the long shape of the Beast glided past.

Summoning the power of his golden boots, Tom knifed up through the water, gaining speed. Shooting up from the surface, he soared over the unsuspecting Beast. He caught hold of Plexor's long neck and flung the chain around the Beast's muzzle.

Using the gills as handholds, Tom scrambled up onto the back of the Beast's skull, pulling the chains tight to clamp Plexor's mouth shut.

The Beast let out a stifled screech of anger. Tom spread his feet, clung onto the chain and prepared himself.

The Beast writhed in the water, sending up fountains of foam as he fought to dislodge Tom. But Tom gritted his teeth and planted his feet ever more firmly on the scales, wrenching at the chain and shifting his balance as the great head swung and swooped and the muffled roars filled his ears.

You won't throw me off this time!
he thought, yanking on the chains to
twist the Beast's head towards the
shoreline. But Plexor dragged his
great head around and dived down
below the surface.

Tom took a huge breath and clung

on grimly as the surface of the water smashed against him.

Deeper and deeper the enraged Beast swam, the water buffeting Tom and almost ripping him off his feet.

He's going to try and force me off for lack of air! Tom realised.

Already his lungs were stinging. Could he hold out? He saw the feathery gills opening and closing at Plexor's neck, and he had an idea. He loosened the chain briefly and drew it back so that it looped over the gills. Then he pulled tight again, clamping the gills closed.

He projected his thoughts through the red jewel at the Beast. *Now neither of us can breathe.*

Plexor whipped and spun in the

water, his shrieks of rage filling Tom's head.

We'll see which of us lasts the longest! Tom roared at the Beast with his mind.

His lungs burned. Lights flashed in front of his eyes.

I must hold on! thought Tom.

Plexor shot upwards in a wild panic. His great head broke the surface close to the harbour, punching up out of the water, sending splintered boats spinning through the air.

With sweet, fresh air filling his lungs at last, Tom heaved on the chains, forcing Plexor to race forward. The Beast crashed into the jetties, as watching villagers ran to get out of the way.

The Beast's great dark body came to a slithering halt in the sand, by the harbour. Tom could sense the Beast's agony and fear through the red jewel as it lay stranded. Villagers began to edge closer, murmuring with fear and wonder. Tom held up a palm. "Stay back!" he shouted.

Tom leaped forwards, his sword drawn. The Orb of Tangala glowed greeny-gold in the defeated Beast's eye socket. The other eye rolled helplessly.

Tom touched the point of his sword to the Orb. *Surrender, Plexor*, he ordered. *Don't prolong your agony*.

The good eye turned upwards, looking at him in anguish.

I surrender, came the Beast's reply.
The huge creature shuddered, and
the scales melted away from under
Tom's feet. With a final quake, Plexor
vanished, exiled from Tangala again.
Tom dropped lightly into the sand.

The Orb of Tangala lay at the water's edge. As Tom stooped and picked it up, he heard a crack of thunder and felt the first drops of rain on his skin. He tilted his head up. Dark clouds were rolling across the sky, and the rain came down in great, heavy swathes. He closed his eyes, enjoying the feel of the cool water on his skin.

The Beast had been defeated and the rains had come to Aran!

9

TREACHERY!

Delighted villagers surrounded Tom, singing and shouting and dancing in the pelting rain.

"You are the great hero!" one cried as they closed in on him.

"He caught the real Cursed Fish and brought the rains!" shouted another, catching Tom's hands and spinning him around until he was dizzy. "The wells will fill again – our cattle will drink! We will survive after all!"

Elenna and Rotu pushed through the throng towards Tom, Silver at Elenna's side and Cory and Emiri coming up behind, leading Storm by the reins.

Rotu slapped Tom on the back. "Truly you are the Master of Beasts!" he said.

"You played your part as well, Prince Rotu," Tom replied, his face burning with embarrassment. That kind of praise always made him feel awkward. "You subdued Plexor in the first battle." He put his hand on the prince's shoulder. "You've proved yourself. Now we will face the final Beast together."

Rotu turned his head, looking away. His cheeks reddened as though he felt somehow shamed by Tom's kind words.

"Now we shall carry our hero in triumph to the village!" cried one of the villagers.

Tom backed off. "There's no need," he said. "Defeating Beasts is my duty, and my honour. I do not need anything more."

The villagers turned towards Rotu instead. "Carry him!" they cried, lifting the prince off his feet and bearing him away on their shoulders.

Elenna stood at Tom's side with Cory, Emiri and the animals, watching the merry procession wind its way up into the village.

"He did well," Elenna said. "Another Beast defeated – and another yet to be found. If only I hadn't lost the map."

Tom turned, gazing across the

lake to the clump of trees where he thought he had seen a cloaked and hooded figure. The same sense of unease shivered through him again. Had it been an illusion?

"I'm going to the nearest well," said Elenna. "We need to refill our water skins for the next stage of the journey. I'll take Storm to the stables first for some food and rest." She took Storm's reins and led the horse away, Silver trotting at her side.

"How will you know where to go without your map?" Emiri asked.

"Elenna has studied the map closely," Tom replied. "I'm sure she'll remember the way to the next Beast." He hoped he was right. They still had to find the sceptre of Pania and return all four of the precious crown jewels to the Royal Palace before King Hugo, Aduro and Daltec were convicted of being involved in their theft. Tom knew that the safety of both the realms was at stake.

If we don't succeed, there will be war between Avantia and Tangala, he thought grimly.

Cory tugged on Tom's sleeve. "Is this the map you were talking about?" he asked, pointing to a bag that had been left on the rain-soaked ground. A roll of paper jutted from the open mouth of the bag.

Cory crouched down and pulled the rolled-up paper from the bag,

opening it between his hands. Rain
splashed down onto the ancient map
of Tangala.

"That's Rotu's bag," Tom said,
frowning thoughtfully.

*How could Prince Rotu have the
map?* It made no sense.

Tom's heart almost stopped as a

sudden realisation struck him.

Back in the desert, he and Elenna had been tormented by strange, vivid hallucinations. But although Rotu said he had also been seeing things, when they met him later in the village, he had seemed perfectly clear-headed.

Tom's head spun. He and Elenna had not begun to hallucinate until after they had taken a drink from the water skin that Rotu had given back to them.

"He put something in the water," Tom muttered, his anger rising as the truth dawned on him. But why would the prince have wanted to drug them?

Tom could only think of one

answer to that question.

"Rotu has been working against us from the very beginning!"

10

THE FACE OF EVIL

Tom's heart sank further as he remembered something that Emiri had said when they first met up with Rotu in the village. "Where has your father gone?" she had asked the prince. Rotu had said she was talking nonsense.

Now Tom turned to Emiri. "Did Rotu come to Aran with another person?" he asked anxiously.

"I think so," Emiri replied uncertainly. "He was with a man wearing a cloak and a hood – and his face was very angry."

A stab of fear entered Tom's chest as he saw again in his mind the figure skulking among the trees when Rotu captured Plexor.

A dreadful thought entered his mind. "No…" he gasped. *It can't be*.

He spun around. Rotu and the villagers had vanished among the houses. He had to find the prince and learn the truth!

But then he heard a far-off howl.

"Silver!" he cried. The howl must mean Elenna was in danger.

Drawing his sword, Tom raced through the outskirts of the village, heading for the well. His golden leg armour gave him extra speed, but when he came to the well, there was no sign of Elenna or the animals.

Where were they? What had happened to them?

He heard another lonely howl.

Is that Silver? He stared around. *Where is he?* The wolf's voice was echoing strangely.

Tom ran to the well and stared down. His heart almost stopped as he saw Elenna treading water deep down the shaft. Silver was swimming around her, whining pitifully.

"I'll get you out," Tom shouted down the well.

Elenna stared up at him and panic swept over her face. "Behind you!"

she screamed. A shadow fell over
Tom as he turned. But before he had
time to defend himself, something
struck him across the side of his
head. He staggered to the lip of the
well, lost his balance and tumbled

down into the deep water.

His head ringing from the blow, Tom swam up to the surface to see a face grinning down at him.

"Rotu!" Tom shouted, treading water at Elenna's side. "Why have you betrayed us?"

Rotu lifted his arm. The Orb of Tangala was in his hand. "Why do you think, you dolt?" Rotu called down. "Thank you for the three Treasures," he added, his voice filled with spiteful sarcasm. "I helped myself from the horse's saddlebag. I knew you wouldn't mind."

"If you've hurt him…" raged Tom.

"Calm yourself," said Rotu. "The animal is locked up in the village."

A second face appeared at Rotu's

side. A cruel, sneering face filled with evil. A face that Tom had hoped he would never see again.

"Velmal!" cried Elenna as Silver let out a growl.

"Your part in these Quests is done, boy," Velmal called down. "The prince and I are going to find the final Beast and return to the Royal City with it." A smile flickered across his face, sharp as a knife. "The people there will be no match for Quagos."

"You can't do that!" shouted Tom.

"You fool, haven't you realised the truth yet?" called Velmal, raising his hand and showing Tom a black jewel he held. "I gave the four Treasures of Tangala to the Beasts so that they would do my bidding. This is the fifth

Treasure of Tangala. It has the power to control any Beast who holds one of the other four."

"This whole Quest was just a trap!" exclaimed Tom.

"The truth dawns at last!"Velmal mocked. "While the Beasts laid in wait for you, Tangala and Avantia would come closer and closer to war. Poor little Beast Master – if only your brain were as sharp as your sword! But it is too late now. Swim while you can, my friends – you will never come out of that well alive."

Tom turned his gaze to Rotu. "How could you do this?" he cried, his voice echoing in the throat of the well.

A smile stretched across the prince's face. "Because Velmal will

make me King of Tangala," he said.
"It's time for Queen Aroha to step
aside – she always was weak-willed
and soft-hearted." He balled his
hands into fists. "Tangala deserves a
strong king who will keep the likes
of you out of the realm!"

"Goodbye, Master of the Beasts," called Velmal, placing an arm around Rotu's shoulder. They both disappeared out of sight.

"Rotu!" shouted Tom. "Don't do this! Velmal is not your friend! Remember my words!"

The faint sound of laughter echoed down to them.

Tom scanned the walls, seeking some kind of footholds. They had to get out of there! If Velmal loosed a Beast on the city of Pania, no one would be safe from his evil power.

"Hear me, Velmal!" Tom shouted desperately. "While there's blood in my veins, I will find a way to defeat you – I swear it!"

CONGRATULATIONS, YOU HAVE COMPLETED THIS QUEST!

At the end of each chapter you were awarded a special gold coin. The QUEST in this book was worth an amazing 11 coins.

Look at the Beast Quest totem picture inside the back cover of this book to see how far you've come in your journey to become

MASTER OF THE BEASTS.

The more books you read, the more coins you will collect!

Do you want your own Beast Quest Totem?
1. Cut out and collect the coin below
2. Go to the Beast Quest website
3. Download and print out your totem
4. Add your coin to the totem
www.beastquest.co.uk/totem

Don't miss the next exciting Beast Quest book, QUAGOS THE ARMOURED BEETLE!

Read on for a sneak peek...

CHAPTER ONE

SPRINGING THE TRAP

Tom's voice was hoarse from shouting for help. The water in the well was icy and the cold seeped into his bones. His legs ached from treading water.

A musty underground smell filled the narrow space around him, and smooth, curved brick rose up on every side. High above Tom's head, a pale circle of sky outlined the shape of a bucket hanging from a rope.

Beside him, Elenna shivered violently, her head bobbing in the water, and her hands making ripples as she paddled. Silver whimpered as he swam in circles to stay afloat.

"We can't wait here until one of the villagers finds us," Tom said. "Rotu and Velmal will be long gone by then. There has to be a way out of here!"

The Evil Wizard and treacherous prince were getting further away by the moment. And with them went the

magical crown jewels of Pania that
Tom and Elenna had fought three
Beasts to recover.

Elenna glanced at Silver. "I don't
think Silver can swim for much
longer. We have to get out of here.
But the walls look too smooth to
climb."

"I could use the power of my
golden boots, if only there was some
solid ground to jump from." Tom
said. Desperately, he looked about
himself, as if a ledge might suddenly
appear – but all he could see was red
brick, and crumbling mortar...

Hmmm. The cracks in the mortar
were barely deep enough for a

fingertip. *But I have to try.*

"I've got an idea," Tom said. "Keep Silver away from the walls. I don't want to fall on either of you."

Elenna beckoned Silver. "What are you going to do?"

"I'm going to try and climb out, but I don't know if I can."

Tom swam to the wall of the well, and scanned the brick. He found a chink in the mortar and dug his freezing fingertips into the crack.

Read QUAGOS THE ARMOURED BEETLE to find out more!

Discover the new Beast Quest mobile game from

Available free on iOS and Android

  **amazon**.com

Guide Tom on his Quest to free the Good Beasts of
Avantia from Malvel's evil spells.

DOWNLOAD THE APP TO BEGIN THE ADVENTURE NOW!

* How to unlock your exclusive shield!

1. Visit www.beast-quest.com/mobilegamesecret

2. Type in the code 2511920

3. Follow the instructions on screen to reveal your exclusive shield